Everyone kept their houses nice and neat,
their front porches spick-and-span,
and the street shipshape.

Every day, Emily Green and her parents
scrubbed and dusted and polished until their
whole house sparkled, from top to bottom.

EMILY GREEN'S GARDEN

Penny Harrison · Megan Forward

Emily Green lived in a perfectly lovely
house, in a perfectly lovely street.

It was the **kind** of street where
people were always busy and
bustling, hurried and hustling.

It was perfectly lovely.

But Emily Green was tired of being neat and tidy. She wanted to play and explore and create.

She wanted to make some mess.

Then, one day, as she swept the pavement outside, a flicker of green caught her eye.

There, growing between the pavers, was a tiny seedling.

Emily Green felt a spark of curiosity.

The next day, she came home from the library with a pile of books and gathered everything she would need.

Carefully, she pulled the seedling
from the ground and planted it.

Slowly, the little seedling grew.

And so did the spark in Emily Green.

At first, her parents were delighted.

'What beautiful shades of green,' her mother said.

'Smells charming in here,' her father said.

Emily Green was enchanted.

She burrowed her fingers in the dirt to plant seeds.

She plucked berries to eat in bed and
flowers to wear in her hair.

She hid among the leaves.

But, before long, she started to develop some peculiar habits.

And, as time passed, her
ideas grew wilder.

Even some of the neighbours
were complaining.

Finally, Emily Green's parents decided ...

the garden had to go.

'We just don't have the room,'
her mother said.

'This kind of garden belongs
outside,' her father said.

Emily Green looked through the
window to the street outside.

She remembered the little seedling she had
found growing between the cracks.

And she wondered.

The next morning, Emily Green and her parents scrubbed and dusted and polished until their whole house sparkled, from top to bottom.

Then they stepped out into the street.

Please take some

No-one was busy and bustling.

No-one looked hurried or hustling.

Instead, children played happily with each other,
people sat and chatted,
and neighbours sipped cups of tea in the morning sun.

It was perfectly ...

lovely.